ALSO BY STEVE WILEY

The Fairytale Chicago of Francesca Finnegan

A Beard Tangled in Dreams: The True Story of Rip Van Winkle

The Imagined Homecoming of Icarus Isakov

GW00492560

Ordering Information:

Quantity sales. Special discounts are available on quantity purchases by bookstores, corporations, associations, and others. For details, contact the publisher at the email address above.

Orders by U.S. trade bookstores and wholesalers may also order directly from Ingram Spark.

Paperback ISBN: 978-1-7353046-4-9

Hardback ISBN: 978-1-7353046-5-6

THE STRANGE STARRY NIGHT

THIS IS THE STORY OF A STORY.

That is to say, the tale herein is derived from another — that of a painting. That particular painting was an interpretation. So, one could also say that this book is an interpretation of an interpretation. An interpretation is the action of explaining meaning. At the risk of overcomplicating the matter, that would make this book a menagerie of meaning.

But meaning should come later in a story. Much later. Let us instead begin with what our reader already knows. The painting. Everyone knows it. The painting decorates museums, beautifies coffee mugs, adorns umbrellas. It covers walls. It covers books. It covers this book. It is ubiquitous. There is even a *Starry Night* Lego set.

That painting tells a story, as does every painting. These stories are often the most imposing of mysteries. Countless works of art have mysterious origins and symbolism. What forgotten peoples painted the Lascaux Cave long ago? What hidden meaning lies within *The Last Supper*? Who was *The Girl with the Pearl Earring*? Who was *The Mona Lisa*?

Vincent Van Gogh's *The Starry Night* is among the most enigmatic of paintings. The story behind its creation is mystifyingly tragic. The tortured artist painted the landscape from his studio within a mental institution in the summer of 1889. He had recently been admitted after cutting off his left ear. After finishing the painting, Van Gogh thought it a failure. He would die of a self-inflicted gunshot wound one year after painting it, having sold just one painting in his lifetime. *The Starry Night* remained in private collection obscurity for decades before landing in New York City's Museum of Modern Art. Today, that 'failure' is deemed priceless. It has become the most recognizable landscape in art history.

Stranger still, we will never truly know what Van Gogh saw in the sky that night. The starry nights have been replaced with electric lights. Were one to observe that French countryside today from the same view Van Gogh held back then, it would look entirely different. Today, there is much less of the starry sky to stir the soul.

In fact, the typical evening sky from just one hundred years ago would be totally unrecognizable today. This point was proven shortly after the 1994 earthquake in Los Angeles. Afterwards, much of the electrical grid was down for two days. The city went dark. Police and emergency services received hundreds of calls from residents wondering whether the appearance of a mysterious, silver cloud in the sky had caused the earthquake.

That 'silver cloud' was the Milky Way. The sight of it had been lost to human memory.

The painting itself is also strange, being almost entirely fantastical. Van Gogh painted it from memory and imagination, something he rarely did. The stars shine with an unnatural radiance. The crescent moon glows bright as the midday sun. The clouds and wind swirl in the sky as if alive. The galaxy flows like a river over the rolling blue hills.

The sleepy village within the painting may be the strangest element of all. That is because there was no sleepy village, at least not from the view Van Gogh held looking out of his asylum window. The village of Saint-Rémy-de-Provence was nearby, and while it is thought the village in the painting is Saint-Rémy, that has never been certain. Some believe the village to be a recollection of Van Gogh's Dutch homeland or another village entirely.

This story of a story takes place within that conjured village on that fateful midsummer night which inspired the painting. It follows the last lamplighter on a journey as wonderfully colored as the painting itself. The village was not at all sleepy on that night. It was alive, with all the real and surreal beauty of the starry sky above.

SAINT-PAUL MENTAL ASYLUM, SAINT-RÉMY-DE-PROVENCE, FRANCE, JUNE 1889

"YOU CANNOT PAINT."

Proclaimed the voice to Vincent Van Gogh, a newly arrived patient at the Saint-Paul Asylum for the mentally ill. Vincent recognized the voice. It was a special voice. It was the only voice he could hear through the side of his head where his left ear had been, before he'd cut it off and gifted it to a prostitute.

It was the voice in his head.

Vincent had just finished dinner. He corked what was left of his red wine ration[1] and rose from the table. He hurried from the dining hall with his head down, the voices from all around indistinguishable from the one in his head. Vincent made for the garden, his sanctuary and source of inspiration. It was a windy afternoon. Vincent hoped the voice of the swaying plants might overwhelm the one in his head.

Vincent slowed down once he reached the old, pillared corridor. He liked that corridor. It dated from the eleventh century when the asylum had first been built as a monastery. It had been transformed into a psychiatric asylum by Franciscan monks in the seventeenth century and was still run by the religious order. Nuns tended the facility and patients, helping to create a comforting atmosphere.

Vincent was relieved at the sight of the garden, and it was a sight. Being midsummer, it was blooming with every color imaginable. He followed the slender stone path to his favorite bench, which sat below a row of pine trees. The trees bent back and forth, wailing a welcome in the wind.

Vincent removed a clay pipe from his pocket to smoke and quiet his mind. He needed a light. Patients were not allowed matches, for obvious reasons. He looked around the garden for someone willing to help. He signaled to the carriage driver. The carriage driver had helped him before and would help him again on that day.

Vincent thanked the man, who after some pleasantries hurried away on some carriage-driving errand. The artist closed his eyes and puffed mindfully. He tilted his head back, listening as the wind composed garden lullabies with its shuffling of the leaves and rippling of the grass.

Shadows danced heavily upon Vincent's tired eyelids. He inhaled the smoke deeply, closed his eyes gently, and was so relaxed he may have soon fallen asleep. Until he heard the voice again.

"You cannot paint."

Vincent jerked his head forward in dismay. He had expected the garden to quiet the voice. It often did.

Vincent finished smoking and rose from the bench. He would go to the common area next. The common area was a simple, square room surrounded by benches fixed to the walls. Its windows overlooked the garden. In the middle of the room was a wood burning stove to gather around.

Vincent could finish his wine in the common area. Perhaps a familiar face would keep him company. The artist was not friendly with many of the patients, most far crazier than him. He was acquainted with many of the staff. Some gathered in the common room. Their chatter might help to quiet the voice in his head.

Vincent found a newly arrived patient his only company in the room. A new patient was a rare and curious thing, there being only about twenty other male patients in the asylum at the time. Vincent examined the patient carefully and cautiously as though he had just happened upon a wild, exotic animal.

The new patient was a teenage boy. Vincent wondered whatever in the world could drive someone so young so mad. Vincent was a doddering thirty-six, after all. The artist felt the mid-thirties was a much more common and respectable age to lose one's mind.

The boy looked quite deranged. He sat in a corner with his knees to his chest, rocking slowly back and forth, mumbling incoherently. Unfortunately for Vincent, the mumbling was not enough to drown out the voice in his head.

"You cannot paint."

Vincent drank the remainder of his wine and hurried from the room. He was headed for the library. Vincent was a voracious reader. A book had the power to transport him to another world entirely. In that world, the voice in his head would be someone else's.

The library was a small, office-sized room. Vincent was pleased to find it empty of patients. He perused the shelves, looking over the familiar lowbrow volumes and religious works stocked by the nuns. Vincent had hoped against hope there would be something new available, something unexpected, but that was not to be.

Vincent left the library empty-handed, intending

to settle on the Shakespeare his brother had recently sent him. He climbed the stairs to his room on the second floor where he hoped an evening of reading and rest awaited him. He walked slowly down the long corridor to his room, imagining the hallway his own private art gallery, when the voice interrupted him again.

"You cannot paint."

Vincent entered his room knowing there was only one sure way to silence the voice in his head, the one that insisted he could not paint. He must paint.

He made his way to the barred bedroom window for inspiration. His room held a fine view of the expansive countryside, flecked with farmhouses. Vincent knew the view well. He had painted it often, always during the day. As the sun began to set, he considered for the first time a rendering of the night.

Vincent stood at the window, staring thoughtfully through the steel bars as the first stars of that historic night blinked to life. There was the half-moon, creeping up from behind the hills. The wind rose with such splendid force, he could almost see it. Trees swayed here and there, always reaching back up to the ether. A lone lantern shone eerily from the hills like a will-o'-the-wisp.

There was no village in sight, but Vincent imagined one. It was a quaint village, not unlike the neighbouring Saint-Rémy. Maybe it was Saint-Rémy. There were cottages doused in moonlight, each of their distant windows coloured with candlelight. There was a church spire rising from the heart of town because every village has a church. The village was sleepy, but not at all dead. There were people there. Who were they? What did they do? What goes on in a village on such a summer night?

Vincent would never know. He was a painter, not a storyteller.

The sky darkening, Vincent hurriedly set up his easel and palette. He was not allowed fire in the room, so he had precious little time to begin his vision of the night. With a dip of his brush into a midnight blue oil, he started the painting of that legendary landscape.

The moment he began the voice in his head was put to rest, and his imagination awoke.

THE VILLAGE IN THE MOONLIGHT.

THAT WAS WHAT VINCENT'S BROTHER THEO CALLED *THE Starry Night*. Theo assumed that village to be Saint-Rémy-de-Provence. So will we. Saint-Rémy was quite literally old as the hills which encircled it. Before the French lived there, the Romans did. Before the Romans lived there, the Celts did. Before the Celts was another tribe so ancient its name and language has been lost to history.

The village had always been mystical. The Celts built a shrine around a spring in a nearby valley and worshipped it for its healing powers. The Romans built a sacred well for the same purpose. The nearby Saint-Paul Asylum was a thousand-year-old monastery. Saint-Rémy was also the birthplace of that infamous seer, Nostradamus.

In Van Gogh's time, the village would have been typical of those in the region. Crooked, medieval streets meandered throughout. A network of canals supported the agriculture surrounding the village, which would have included olive groves, fruit farms, and vineyards. The Alpilles Mountains lorded over the village and countryside.

The village was small, with no more than a few thousand inhabitants. Most would have been commoners: farmers, fisherman, tradesman. The social gathering place was the tavern. The spiritual gathering place was the church. Everyone would have known everyone.

In that village lived the last lamplighter.

Not that he was the last lamplighter *ever*. He was the last lamplighter for the village of Saint-Rémy. That notorious starry night would be his last one on the job. The town was scheduled to be wired with a new and innovative technology called 'electricity' the following day. The technological revolution had arrived. Oil fires would be replaced with electric bulbs. The lamplighters would be replaced with switch-flickers.

The name of the last lamplighter was Lucas. Lucas had grown up in the village, as had his father, and his father before him. His father had been the lamplighter, as had his father before him.

Lucas took great pride in being a lamplighter. That job might seem menial today, but back then it was a respected career. The lamplighter didn't simply light the night. He brought a measure of solace and safety to all who walked the streets after dark.

Lucas looked like a street lamp. He was tall and skinny, standing straight and rigid as a pole. His dark hair and lampshade mustache were a coal black. His eyes were a smoldering shade of grey. He wore a raggedy straw hat like a rain shield. He had a friendly face and disposition.

Lucas was a simple man. Like most with solitary occupations, he kept mostly to himself. When he wasn't lighting lamps, he was raising his only daughter, Amelia. Amelia was just eight years old. Her mother and wife to Lucas had been named Chloe.

Chloe had tragically died the winter before from one of those rampant, now curable ailments of the age: Polio. Polio outbreaks had become more frequent beginning in the late-nineteenth century. Chloe was paralyzed with the infectious disease for a short while before succumbing. Lucas and Amelia were left a fractured family, all alone in the world.

Lucas was a minimalist. He had no choice in the matter. A lone lamplighter had little disposable income. A widowed lamplighter with a daughter had next to nothing. Lucas's wages earned him just enough for sustenance and shelter. Lucas and Amelia lived in a threadbare, thatched cottage. They wore simple clothing. They ate simple fare. They drank water from the well. They drank watered-down wine.

But the life of our lamplighter was not only one of trial and tribulation. The fondest of memories cost nothing at all. Playing, joking, laughing. *Dancing*. Amelia danced. She was like her mother in that way. Chloe would dance her way out of bed in the morning. She would dance in the sun, wind, and rain. She would dance with a broom, sweeping the cottage floor. Polio is the most insidious of ailments for a dancer. The disease would gradually paralyze Chloe, robbing her of the ability to dance. Soon after, it would rob her of the will to live.

Chloe would dance with Lucas as he tended the garden. Lucas was always tending the garden. If Lucas had not inherited the village lamplighter title from his father (and his father before him), he would have been a gardener. Lucas's garden was recognized as the finest in Saint-Rémy. It was a small, colorful orchard containing only the sweetest of fruits. There were apples, figs, pears, cherries, peaches, and apricots. His pomegranate tree was the only one in town. Lucas was generous with its harvest.

Gardening was a hobby for Lucas. Lamp-lighting was a profession. Our reader may presume one working such an unskilled trade to be slow-witted. While other lamplighters may have fit that description, Lucas did not. He was an avid reader in a time and place when a small fraction of men of his societal position were literate. The bookseller rolled his rickety cart into the village market the last Sunday of each month. Lucas would scrounge up just enough for one new book, maybe two.

Lucas read and reread the great-great-grandfathers of modern fantasy. He collected the works of Hans Christian Anderson, George MacDonald, H.G. Wells, and Lewis Carroll, all of whom were popular at the time. Jules Verne was his favorite. Being French, Verne was the most accessible and least costly. Lucas read poetry but only of the imagined kind. His translation of *A Midsummer Night's Dream* was one of his most treasured belongings.

Lucas's imagination brought those fantastical tales along with him on his nightly excursions to illuminate the village. Shadows from the lamps came to life as dwarfs, demons, and dragons. The phantom beings walked the silent streets with him, keeping him company. Lucas lit the lamps dutifully every single night of the year as though he were responsible for lighting the stars themselves. When the night was fully dark, he saw in the stars all those heroes and monsters of legend. The wind whistled their tales, and Lucas listened.

Lucas's days of conjuring spirits from the starlight

would soon be at an end. He was the last lamplighter, and it was his last night of work. The lamps of the village would soon be lit by some all-powerful switchman. Lucas would be out of the only job he had ever known. He wondered what became of a lamplighter with no lamps to light.

...the Rabbit actually took a watch out of its waistcoat-pocket, and looked at it, and then hurried on, Alice started to her feet, for it flashed across her mind that she had never before seen a rabbit with either a waistcoat-pocket, or a watch to take out of it, and burning with curiosity, she ran across the field after it, and fortunately was just in time to see it pop down a large rabbit-hole under the hedge.

In another moment down went Alice after it, never once considering how in the world she was to get out again.

The rabbit-hole went straight on like a tunnel for some way, and then dipped suddenly down, so suddenly that Alice had not a moment to think about stopping herself before she found herself falling down a very deep well.

Either the well was very deep, or she fell very slowly, for she had plenty of time as she went down to look about her and to wonder what was going to happen next. First, she tried to look down and make out what she was coming to, but it was too dark to see anything; then she looked at the sides of the well, and noticed that they were filled with cupboards and book-shelves; here and there she saw maps and pictures hung upon pegs. She took down a jar from one of the shelves as she passed; it was labelled "ORANGE MARMALADE", but to her great disappointment it was empty: she did not like to drop the jar for fear of killing somebody underneath, so managed to put it into one of the cupboards as she fell past it.

"Well!" thought Alice to herself, "after such a fall as this, I shall think nothing of tumbling down stairs!

How brave they'll all think me at home! Why, I wouldn't say anything about it, even if I fell off the top of the house!" (Which was very likely true.)

~ *Lewis Carroll, Alice in Wonderland, 1865*

SOME SECRET REALMS LAY AT THE BOTTOM OF RABBIT HOLES. Others sit behind magic mirrors. Some are happened upon within dusty old wardrobes while playing hide-and-seek. Sometimes, what seems a simple door is an entryway to another dimension. In the case of our lamplighter, that once-upon-a-time-portal passed through a tavern, with the help of a green fairy.

You see, Lucas's last night of labor began without any labor at all. It began with drinks at the village tavern. After all, it was his last night of work. That was cause for celebration.

One can see the tavern quite clearly in *The Starry Night*. It is the property just below the church with the two candlelit windows. That place is obviously a tavern because it is nearest to the church. In olden days, taverns were often situated near churches due to the fact that places of worship were generally located at the center of town. The center of town was of course the busiest and best location for an establishment serving thirsty townsfolk and travelers.

After he had put his daughter to bed, Lucas began his shift at the village tavern for what locals and the rest of France referred to as the 'green hour.' Green hour was the ancestor to the modern-day happy hour. It was named green after the color of the type of alcohol consumed – absinthe – also known as the 'green fairy.'

Absinthe was hugely popular in nineteenth-century France. It was the drink of choice for nearly every societal class. Bohemians were especially fond of it. Van Gogh himself was a frequent absinthe drinker. The telltale, champagne-shaped absinthe glass features in many of his paintings.

Absinthe is perhaps best known for its hallucinogenic properties. Drinkers have reported psychedelic, mind-altering effects. Artists praised absinthe as a consciousness-expanding, creative stimulus. Its only downside was the occasional psychosis. Because of that unfortunate side-effect, absinthe was eventually banned in most of Europe and the United States.

Absinthe wasn't banned that night. It flowed from bottles to glasses to mouths like a roaring river of emerald. Lucas was welcomed to the tavern with a hearty chalice of it. He would not have to pay for the many drinks he drank that night. All in the village were aware of it being the lamplighters final night on the job.

"A fine night for a last light!" the postman slapped Lucas on the back.

"These so-called 'electric' street lamps are the design of Lucifer," declared an old codger. "The demonic contrivances won't work for more than a fortnight. You'll be back on the job in no time, no time at all."

"Paris has been wired with the electricity now ten years[1]," pointed out the blacksmith.

"If these mechanical street lamps do work, what will you do with the time?" asked the postman.

"Sleep!" Lucas joked, raising his glass for a toast.

In truth, the question was one Lucas had asked himself countless times. What would he do for work? He had no other craft and few practical skills. He could read and write, but that did him little good. Saint-Rémy was not Paris. There were few jobs for readers and writers. He *could* garden. That was practical. He wondered if he might find work as a gardener or farmhand.

Lucas drank his cares away along with what was left of his glass. Green hour was no time for the worries of work or anything else. It was the time for a whirl with the green fairy. She summoned him from the bar. He would answer her call, again and again.

THE FIRST GREEN HOUR ENDED WITH A DECISION BY ALL IN attendance that there should be a second green hour. The second green hour would further honor Lucas, the last and greatest lamplighter of the era.

The second hour was much like the first but with song and dance. One or two prostitutes joined in the celebration, hoping to steal away one or two of the more vulnerable men. By the second hour, the absinthe began to taste different to Lucas. In the first hour, it tasted how it always did – biting, bitter, vitriolic. Disgusting. In the second hour it tasted less disgusting. In fact, it tasted like hardly anything at all. That, of course, was the problem. Lucas was accustomed to a glass or two of absinthe, not three, or four, or more.

The psychoactive compound in the absinthe began to take effect. Green hour began to look green.

The bartender had transformed into a hobgoblin alchemist, smiling with cunning delight at every new potion he poured. Each of the individual flames within the candlewax chandelier overhead joined hands and danced in a circle. The setting sun cast strange, moving shadows through the west window. They drank and mingled with the rest.

Lucas was snapped out of his trance by the surprisingly sober miller.

"When will you get to work?" the miller asked.

When would he get to work? Night was darkening the village and without any lamps lit. How would the townsfolk find their way through the unlighted alleyways? How would the commerce of evening commence? What fire would keep banditry at bay, confined to the shadows?

Lucas drained the last of his glass and headed stealthily for the door. Any pronouncement of his leaving would undoubtedly be met with objections from the raucous crowd.

The school teacher spied Lucas before he made his escape. The man climbed onto the bar to speak.

"Lucas, a ballad before you set forth on your closing crusade of twilight?"

All cheered in drunken enthusiasm. The teacher opened a small book of verse. He read *The Lamplighter* by Robert Louis Stevenson, which had just been published a few years earlier.

My tea is nearly ready and the sun has left the sky;
  It's time to take the window to see Leerie[2] going by;
    For every night at teatime and before you take your seat,

With lantern and with ladder he comes posting up
the street.

Now Tom would be a driver and Maria go to sea,
    And my papa's a banker and as rich as he can be;
    But I, when I am stronger and can choose what I'm
to do,
    Oh Leerie, I'll go round at night and light the
lamps with you!

For we are very lucky, with a lamp before the door,
    And Leerie stops to light it as he lights so many
more;
    And O! before you hurry by with ladder and with
light,
    O Leerie, see a little child and nod to him tonight!

The tavern howled in approval. The teacher bowed in appreciation. Lucas smiled a farewell. His last night of work awaited.

THE WIND ROARED TO GREET LUCAS AS HE STEPPED outside, reawakening his dimmed senses. They call that wind the mistral in France. It is no ordinary wind. The mistral is a mighty, northwesterly wind that blows from southern France along the Rhone River Valley to the Mediterranean Sea.

Lucas grabbed hold of his trusty lamplighter's pole. He ignited a match with the subtle snap of his fingers. The snapping match was a parlor trick he'd learned from his father (and his father before him). It was quite convenient for someone lighting fires so frequently.

LAMPLIGHTER'S POLE LIT, LUCAS MADE HIS WAY TO THE center of the street to ignite his first lamp. He made it only a few steps. The lamp he intended to light, the one he had lit so many times before, had vanished. Lucas closed his glassy eyes in confusion, thinking himself mad. Reopening them, he saw the lamp was still nowhere to found.

Had the lamp been there when Lucas first arrived to the tavern? The absinthe-induced haze made it difficult to say for sure. He looked down the darkening street to where another lamp normally stood. It too had disappeared.

Lucas wondered how he or anyone would ever return home without lamps to light the way.

Who could that be talking to him? The wind was rising again, and getting very loud, and full of rushes and whistles. He was sure someone was talking—and very near him, too, it was. But he was not frightened, for he had not yet learned how to be; so he sat up and hearkened. At last the voice, which, though quite gentle, sounded a little angry, appeared to come from the back of the bed. He crept nearer to it, and laid his ear against the wall. Then he heard nothing but the wind, which sounded very loud indeed. The moment, however, that he moved his head from the wall, he heard the voice again, close to his ear. He felt about with his hand, and came upon the piece of paper his mother had pasted over the hole. Against this he laid his ear, and then he heard the voice quite distinctly. There was, in fact, a little corner of the paper loose, and through that, as from a mouth in the wall, the voice came.

"What do you mean, little boy—closing up my window?"

"What window?" asked Diamond.

"You stuffed hay into it three times last night. I had to blow it out again three times."

"You can't mean this little hole! It isn't a window; it's a hole in my bed."

"I did not say it was a window: I said it was my window."

"But it can't be a window, because windows are holes to see out of."

"Well, that's just what I made this window for."

"But you are outside: you can't want a window."

"You are quite mistaken. Windows are to see out of,

you say. Well, I'm in my house, and I want windows to see out of it."

"But you've made a window into my bed."

"Well, your mother has got three windows into my dancing room, and you have three into my garret."

"But I heard father say, when my mother wanted him to make a window through the wall, that it was against the law, for it would look into Mr. Dyves's garden."

The voice laughed.

"The law would have some trouble to catch me!" it said.

"But if it's not right, you know," said Diamond, "that's no matter. You shouldn't do it."

"I am so tall I am above that law," said the voice.

"You must have a tall house, then," said Diamond.

"Yes; a tall house: the clouds are inside it."

"Dear me!" said Diamond, and thought a minute. "I think, then, you can hardly expect me to keep a window in my bed for you. Why don't you make a window into Mr. Dyves's bed?"

"Nobody makes a window into an ash-pit," said the voice, rather sadly. "I like to see nice things out of my windows."

"But he must have a nicer bed than I have, though mine is very nice—so nice that I couldn't wish a better."

"It's not the bed I care about: it's what is in it. But you just open that window."

"Well, mother says I shouldn't be disobliging; but it's rather hard. You see the north wind will blow right in my face if I do."

"I am the North Wind."

~ George MacDonald, At the Back of the North Wind, 1865

Lucas wondered where the street lamps had gone.

They could not have up and vanished entirely. They had to have somehow been moved, concluded our absinthe-indulging leerie. Perhaps it was the absinthe that did the moving – in his mind's eye. After all, the green fairy was a trickster known for illusory ruses.

Perhaps it was another fairy altogether. Locals told tales of cursed fairy rings appearing on the hillsides late in the long summer nights. Hedonistic fairy clans would revel under the stars, kidnapping unlucky travelers. Might they have kidnapped a street lamp, or two?

Lucas decided it best to return to the tavern. He would speculate with the drinkers and dancers as to the whereabouts of the lamps over more drinks. Turning away from the street, he was once again taken by surprise, this time by the sight of the shuttered tavern. It looked to have closed for the evening. Lucas wondered where everyone had gone and why the place had suddenly closed. It was normally open until at least midnight. Had he lost track of the time?

"Where has the time gone?" Lucas asked himself out loud.

The wind howled in response, blowing out the flame on Lucas's lamplighter's pole. Lucas stood there, awestruck. Such a thing had never happened to him in all his years on the job. The flame on the tip of his pole was fed from calcium carbide, a chemical compound which generates inflammable gas. Such a flame was nearly impossible to blow out.

Lucas looked up and saw the sky in motion. It seemed to him the wind was swirling to life. It came soaring down into the street, where it formed the shape of a woman. Her seemingly endless hair spread like a patchy fog over the village before settling neatly onto her head.

Lucas had encountered untold numbers of eccentric folk in his lamp-lighting days. One who wanders after dark is bound to. He'd met wayfaring strangers, worldly witches, roving phantoms, rambling phantasms, and more. He once came upon a gypsy crone spit-roasting a cat in an alley under one of his lamps. He lit the lamp and wished her a fine supper.

That is to say, Lucas was accustomed to strange sights in the night. But the wind coming to life was something else entirely. He stood blinking stupidly, trying to make sense of what he was seeing. The wind was certainly a female, that much was certain. Her age was hard to say in the faint moonlight. One moment she was a woman, the next a girl, then an old hag, then a woman again. She finally settled into a lady of middle age, far younger than was possible for an ages-old force of nature like her to be.

"Good evening, Lucas," she greeted. Her voice sounded like a tin whistle.

"A fine evening to you," Lucas replied, as though

the meeting was not at all out of the ordinary. "Might I ask how you know my name?"

"I have known you since you were you. I crept through the cracks in the wall of your nursery when you were still a baby. I waved your hair with the wheat fields you played in as a boy. I have kept you company on these many lonely nights as you wander the streets making light for other wanderers, like me."

She walked closer to him. Her eyes shone a cold, misty grey.

"I am the Mistral," she bowed.

"Indeed, we have met," Lucas acknowledged. "I have known you all these years. I wonder where all those years have gone? Time has gotten away from me on this night, as have my street lamps. It is my duty to light them one last time."

"Time gets away from everyone, though I have never heard of a street lamp having gone missing along with it. I can guess where the time has gone to this night. Perhaps if we make our way in that direction, we will happen upon your misplaced street lamps."

"In that case, lead the way," Lucas agreed. "I should like to find the time at the very least."

THE MISTRAL LED THE WAY DOWN THE UNLIT STREETS. SHE walked like the wind. Her shoulders did not rise and fall. Her long, light hair spread all about her torso like a dress, making it impossible to see her feet, if she had any at all. She walked slowly, then fast. Then slowly again.

Lucas had hoped to come across a stray lamp to

light, to get a better look at his blustery guide. That was not to be. The night grew darker until it was not just black but wraith-like. Stray villagers passed them by. All were in a hurry, holding lanterns to light their way home.

Lucas and the Mistral soon came upon the old, abandoned schoolhouse at the edge of town. It was half-covered in wild ivy, what remained of the original brick exposed on the other half, all weathered and crumbled, mortar gone. The moon rose over the hills, shining through the shattered front window where Lucas found himself looking for something, he knew not what.

"What is time doing at the schoolhouse?" Lucas asked the Mistral.

"Here is where time often gets lost. Primary, secondary, tertiary... Always working, studying, slaving for a tomorrow without a thought for today. Here is a ritualistic slaughtering of meaning in the here and now. More time is forever lost here than anywhere, with the possible exception of the penitentiary. Rest assured, we are sure to find some trace of lost time here."

Lucas followed the Mistral toward the schoolhouse. Everything was expectedly barren. The door was locked and the windows shuttered or broken. The field behind the school was desolate. The merry-go-round spun hauntingly in the wind. The swings swung with the same ghosts.

Then, something caught Lucas's eye. At first, it looked like a wilted tree in the middle of the field behind the school. Upon closer examination, Lucas realized it was a street lamp. How it got there, he had no earthly idea. It was quite out of place. Still, Lucas was determined to light it. It was his duty.

The Mistral followed Lucas as he made his way across the field. Once he reached the errant lamp, he ignited his trusty pole. He carefully reached the torch up as he'd done countless times before. The lamp ignited into a sudden burst of silver flame, casting a light as bright as a boyhood sun over the school grounds.

Lucas squinted in astonishment at the schoolyard. It was no longer a dark and desolate field. The lamplight had transformed it into the lush meadow it once was, waving with grass, brimming with flowers. Lucas stared, images of the past playing upon his senses. Apparitions of children played at hide-and-seek. Some rolled and wrestled through the flowers. Others blew the bulbs off dandelions. He could hear their laughter, free and clear in the night turned day.

The Mistral had found a trace of time from long ago. It was not of the sort of time Lucas had expected to encounter. Still, he was pleased to have found it and would remain there if he could.

The lamp did not shine with lost time for long. Lucas saw her in the moments just before the lamp dimmed and the night returned. There she was, golden hair glowing in the lamplight as she raced across the meadow. And there was a young Lucas! The boy chased playfully after her into the shadows of the trees.

The shimmering lamp cooled to its usual, faint glow. The scene from the past all but disappeared. The schoolchildren vanished with the exception of the girl. She ran away from the field, into the woods.

Lucas knew exactly where she was going – the wishing well.

Lucas knew where the girl was going because he knew the girl, all too well. It was the childhood vision of his former wife, Chloe. Lucas ran excitedly towards her, intending to follow the girl she had been into the woods.

"Fare thee well in the forest, lamplighter," said the knowing Mistral.

"Will you not join me?" Lucas asked. "The night is young, and we have found just one lamp. I should like your help in finding the others."

"No, the trees will not grant me safe passage," explained the Mistral. "I am off to the hills where I may roam free. Our paths are sure to cross again. I wish you well this night."

Her voice trailed away with the whistle of a gathering wind. She grew taller and larger, reaching up and into the sky. Her hair also grew. It grew longer and longer until it splayed across the ether in endless, ashen ripples. Soon she was gone, having dissolved into the night above.

They shut the road through the woods
   Seventy years ago.
   Weather and rain have undone it again,
   And now you would never know
   There was once a road through the woods
   Before they planted the trees.
   It is underneath the coppice and heath,
   And the thin anemones.
   Only the keeper sees
   That, where the ring-dove broods,
   And the badgers roll at ease,
   There was once a road through the woods.

Yet, if you enter the woods
   Of a summer evening late,
   When the night-air cools on the trout-ringed pools
   Where the otter whistles his mate,
   (They fear not men in the woods,
   Because they see so few.)
   You will hear the beat of a horse's feet,
   And the swish of a skirt in the dew,
   Steadily cantering through
   The misty solitudes,
   As though they perfectly knew
   The old lost road through the woods.
   But there is no road through the woods.

~ **Rudyard Kipling, The Way Through the Woods, 1910**

There is indeed a forest in *The Starry Night*. It is little and lurking just behind the village, beneath the blue hills beyond. Those woods were just as ancient as the town. The trees there were the last remaining survivors of a once vast, now forgotten forest. Villagers claimed their roots lined the walls of Satan's bedchamber in the nethermost pits of hell.

Lucas walked into what was left of the primeval forest. The swaying cypresses wailed a welcome (or warning) as he passed under them. He found the trail he'd known as a boy overgrown with roots and reeds. Lucas followed it easily, dark though it was. He could have walked to the well blindfolded, having visited there so often as a boy. The well water served the school, as well as the imagination of its children.

It wasn't long before Lucas reached the well. It looked like a wishing well. It was stony, grimy, and ages-old. The bottom was deeper than deep, somewhere near the center of the earth. It smelled like rotten eggs and wishes. That smell never bothered the children. Those were the days when wishes were fulfilled not by Amazon, but by shooting stars, dandelion bulbs, and of course, wishing wells.

The well reminded Lucas of a night long before, wishing with Chloe when they were children. That was a strange and starry night, not unlike the one Lucas found himself wandering. He had thrown a coin down the well that night. He wished for what every child wishes for; some toy, trinket, or other childish desire. Chloe didn't wish for anything. She never wished for anything because she knew something Lucas didn't. She knew that wishes rarely come true, and she was already rich with the only currency that really matters – time. Most children are.

Lucas searched around the well for the childhood apparition of his wife. There was no sign of her. Had she fallen down the well? Lucas peered into it. At first, he could see nothing, so he snapped a match to life and dropped it down. The well was dry. To his surprise, he saw a lamp at the bottom — a lamp that needed lighting.

Lucas dropped his pole down the well before crawling in himself. The well was lined with thick vines of ivy that he used to climb down. He was nearing the bottom when he lost his grip and fell. He narrowly avoided impaling himself on the lamp, landing squarely but safely on his back.

Lucas reached for his pole to light the lamp, it being expectedly dark at the bottom of the well. The lamp ignited with the same sudden shimmer as the one in the schoolyard. It lit the whole of the well, which turned out to be an immense, cavernous hall. The place was filled with wishes, every single wish ever cast into it.

They were children's wishes mostly because children wish more than anyone. Masses of toys lay about, everything from jack-in-the-boxes to beautiful bisque dolls. The spirits of children themselves wandered about. Many had wings, soaring here and there, smiling, because every child wishes they could fly. Other, older souls embraced. Friends and family separated in the cruel world above reunited in that curious one below. They joined together, singing and dancing. Their voices were strangely distant echoes from the past. There were riches scattered about, wishes of the poor. Chests filled with precious gems and metals lined the walls of the cavern.

Lucas was drawn to the youngest of wishes. Those wishes were the most interesting and imaginative because children wish mostly to wish, to dream anything might be real.

Lucas had often wished into that well as a boy. He searched about hoping he might rediscover one of his own long-lost wishes. He recognized none of the toys or trinkets as his own. The fame and fortune were not his, nor were the wings. He had been as simple a boy as he was a man.

Lucas had not been in the wishing well for long when he came upon something unexpected — another wishing well.

"How strange," he thought aloud, "for a wishing well to be within a wishing well."

It was not at all strange when one considers what the clever child wishes for. That child wishes for more wishes, and there were yet to be granted ones all around the well. They were shiny coins of every shape and age, waiting to be thrown in with some hope or dream.

The soon-to-be-unemployed lamplighter picked one of the coins up, considering what he should wish for. There was so much he hoped for and needed and much else that had been lost. One wish was hardly enough. He picked up another coin and another after that. He picked up coins until his hands were full of them. He dropped the coins into the well.

Then he dropped himself into the well.

One may consider Lucas's leaping down the well an impetuous, if not insane decision. It was not. He followed the wishes to find and realize them. If the wishes died at the bottom of that well within a well, consigned to some subterranean oblivion, that would be his destiny as well. Without his wishes fulfilled, Lucas felt he may as well have been a coin. At least a coin had worth.

Every evening the young Fisherman went out upon the sea, and threw his nets into the water.

When the wind blew from the land he caught nothing, or but little at best, for it was a bitter and black-winged wind, and rough waves rose up to meet it. But when the wind blew to the shore, the fish came in from the deep, and swam into the meshes of his nets, and he took them to the market-place and sold them.

Every evening he went out upon the sea, and one evening the net was so heavy that hardly could he draw it into the boat. And he laughed, and said to himself, 'Surely I have caught all the fish that swim, or snared some dull monster that will be a marvel to men, or some thing of horror that the great Queen will desire,' and putting forth all his strength, he tugged at the coarse ropes till, like lines of blue enamel round a vase of bronze, the long veins rose up on his arms. He tugged at the thin ropes, and nearer and nearer came the circle of flat corks, and the net rose at last to the top of the water.

But no fish at all was in it, nor any monster or thing of horror, but only a little mermaid lying fast asleep.

Her hair was as a wet fleece of gold, and each separate hair as a thread of fine gold in a cup of glass. Her body was as white ivory, and her tail was of silver and pearl. Silver and pearl was her tail, and the green weeds of the sea coiled round it; and like sea-shells were her ears, and her lips were like sea-coral. The cold waves dashed over her cold breasts, and the salt glistened upon her eyelids.

So beautiful was she that when the young fisherman saw her he was filled with wonder, and he put out his hand and drew the net close to him, and leaning over the side he clasped her in his arms. And when he touched her, she gave a cry like a startled sea-gull, and woke, and looked at him in terror with her mauve-amethyst eyes, and struggled that she might escape. But he held her tightly to him, and would not suffer her to depart.

~ *Oscar Wilde, The Fisherman and His Soul, 1891*

LUCAS PLUNGED HEAD FIRST, STRAIGHT DOWN TOWARD whatever was at the bottom of the wishing well. He fell for an impossibly long time. Looking down and around, he tried to ascertain when and where he might finally land. The walls of the well around him gradually disappeared. He was confused by that for only a few seconds before splashing into the water.

Lucas swam quickly to the surface, surprised to see the night above and water below. He realized he was in the middle of a fast-flowing river on the outskirts of town. That river lay hidden between the hills overlooking the village in *The Starry Night*, just beyond the woods and below the sky. The hills were used for farming. The river was used for fishing.

Lucas tried to swim to shore but couldn't. He was tangled within a fishing net. The net was large enough to trawl the full breadth of the river. Lucas would not escape it without help.

"Hello, please! Someone, help!" Lucas shouted as he struggled to free himself.

A shabby rowboat answered his call, an old man paddling it from an even older dock. The old man looked like a river-boat captain. He wore a long, navy blue sailor's pea coat and dark corduroy pants. Strands of silver hair poked through the holes of a raggedy peaked cap. A corncob pipe protruded through his white whiskers.

The mysterious boatman untangled Lucas and helped him aboard.

"Who in the name of Napoleon are you?" the old man asked.

"I... I am Lucas, the village lamplighter," Lucas explained as he caught his breath. "Thank you for pulling me from the river."

"Just what is a lamplighter doing in the middle of the river in the middle of the night?"

"I am on the job," Lucas shook himself dry. "Who are you?"

"I am a fisherman, and also on the job, lucky for you."

"What is a fisherman fishing in the dead of night for?" asked Lucas. "Fishing is best done under a morning sun, or so I've heard."

"Morning *is* best for catching fish, but I'm not fishing for fish. I'm fishing for wishes. Most fisherman fish for wishes, though few realize it. The ordinary fisherman casts his line of hope into the wild blue yonder, hopeful the jaws of fish (or fate) will bite. Fish for long enough and all those wishes of the world can be caught; immortality, transcendence, meaning. One might also catch a simple, common wish. Maybe a girl, or a kiss. Maybe a first kiss, or a last."

Lucas wondered if he were a wish himself, having just thrust himself down a wishing well.

"What is your wish?" Lucas asked.

"I am an old man. I wish what old men wish for. I wish for time long-past and friends long-gone. I wish for the time I don't have and the health I still have."

The fisherman puffed thoughtfully on his pipe. He

sent smoke rings of all shape, size, and color floating low over the river.

"I wish most for a girl gone away," the fisherman continued. "It is her I am fishing for tonight. When I first saw you splashing, I was sure you were her."

"I am sorry to disappoint," said Lucas, thinking of his wife. Of all the wishes he had fallen with into the well, the one for her had been nearest to his heart.

"What does she look like?" Lucas asked.

The old man took off his cap and bowed his head, smoking thoughtfully. He thought of a time long ago where faded memories became indistinguishable from hopes and dreams.

"I only ever saw her at night. She had this endless, pumpkin-orange hair woven through a silver circlet. Her skin was pale as it comes, almost translucent. The jade and silver of her tail glittered like jeweled seaweed when the moon hung low. She had one of those faces worth launching a thousand ships. Her lips were amethyst. Her sapphire eyes twinkled with the stars."

"A mermaid?" guessed Lucas.

"Yes. The consummate seafaring fantasy, the original nautical goddess, the romance of every sailor's shanty. The wish of me and a whole history of mariners."

The fisherman hummed a sea shanty under his breath.

Oh 'twas in the broad Atlantic, mid the equinoctial gales,

That a young fellow fell overboard among the sharks and whales,

And down he went as a streak of light, so quickly down went he,

Until he came to a mermaid at the bottom of the deep blue sea.

"I wish I could help you in the catching of your wish, but I am no fisherman," said Lucas. "I am a lamplighter."

"That you are, yet you may be just what I need. There is a street lamp a short ways downriver. It needs lighting. Its gleaming over the water would help me to fish."

"Why, certainly," Lucas agreed. He was by that point in the night unsurprised at there being a street lamp standing all alone by the riverside, so strangely removed from the village. The night had so far been inexplicable; the remainder would be no different.

THE PAIR ROWED DOWN THE EARTHLY RIVER, ITS PATH following the hazy course of the Milky Way above. The old fisherman gave Lucas a blanket to dry himself of wishes and to shelter him from the cooling Mistral. She blew wildly over the hills and valleys, as promised.

They rowed to a skinny pier where one of the village street lamps stood. It looked quite out of place. The fisherman moored the boat, and the two walked to the lamp. Lucas only then realized he had no matches for a fire or his lamp-lighting pole.

"Here, use my fishing pole to light the lamp," offered the fisherman.

The fisherman tied a matchbook to the end of his

pole with fishing line and handed it to Lucas. Lucas ignited the book with that subtle snap of his fingers, the way he always did. He reached the flaming fishing pole carefully up to the lamp. It ignited, illuminating the river below.

The lamplight revealed strange and secret river creatures. On the water, horse-like kelpie galloped, splashing down the pier and into the surrounding hills. In the water, Lucas saw the faces of serpents scowling at him as they whizzed by toward the open sea. The lamplight seemed to draw the creatures closer to the pier.

The lamp had only just been lit when the fisherman raced to his boat without explanation. He hurriedly leapt in and rowed to the middle of the river. He left in such a hurry, he'd forgotten his fishing pole. Lucas held it up, signaling to him from the pier, but the fisherman took no notice. He was chasing something in the water.

It was the wish he had been fishing for — the mermaid. Lucas saw the jade and silver of her tail glittering in the moonlight, just as he'd described it. The fisherman rowed frantically, pursuing her downriver.

Lucas watched until the pair were faraway and just two specks on the water. He last saw them where the horizon line disappeared, where the darkness of the river joined that of the night. There the fisherman's boat took flight, sailing into the sea of ether above. The mermaid splashed through the stars, always one step ahead of him.

Lucas stood spellbound on the pier, watching the fisherman as he disappeared behind the moon in pursuit of the mermaid. The lamplighter considered the night so far and the strange saga it had been. The wind come to life. Time regained. Wishing wells within wishing wells. Mermaids. He wondered where the evening would take him next.

Lucas intended to return to the village and to normalcy. He hoped to finish his last night of work. The night was no longer young. He had lit only three lamps. There were many more to be lit.

Lucas tripped on the fishing pole as he walked from the pier. It was somehow baited and ready. It was as if the pole were asking for him to use it once more. Lucas agreed, casting a line into the water. He wondered if he might catch one of those elusive wishes.

It wasn't long before there was a tug on the line. Then another. Lucas was unused to such a tug. His heart beat faster with each new pull on the rod. He excitedly pulled back, reeling in the catch as quick as he might. The reeling was easy. Fish or wish, there wasn't much to it.

A simple, silver fish flopped onto the pier. It wasn't the wish Lucas had hoped for, but it was something. He wondered if he could pass for a fisherman once his lamp-lighting days were done. With the old fisherman orbiting the moon, it seemed there was an opportunity.

Puck

How now, spirit! whither wander you?

Fairy

Over hill, over dale, Thorough bush, thorough brier,
Over park, over pale,
Thorough flood, thorough fire,
I do wander everywhere,
Swifter than the moon's sphere;
And I serve the fairy queen,
To dew her orbs upon the green.
The cowslips tall her pensioners be:
In their gold coats spots you see;
Those be rubies, fairy favours,
In those freckles live their savours:
I must go seek some dewdrops here
And hang a pearl in every cowslip's ear.
Farewell, thou lob of spirits; I'll be gone:
Our queen and all our elves come here anon.

Puck

The king doth keep his revels here to-night:
Take heed the queen come not within his sight;
For Oberon is passing fell and wrath,
Because that she as her attendant hath
A lovely boy, stolen from an Indian king;
She never had so sweet a changeling;
And jealous Oberon would have the child
Knight of his train, to trace the forests wild;
But she perforce withholds the loved boy,
Crowns him with flowers and makes him all her joy:

And now they never meet in grove or green,
By fountain clear, or spangled starlight sheen,
But, they do square, that all their elves for fear
Creep into acorn-cups and hide them there.

Fairy

Either I mistake your shape and making quite,
Or else you are that shrewd and knavish sprite
Call'd Robin Goodfellow: are not you he
That frights the maidens of the villagery;
Skim milk, and sometimes labour in the quern
And bootless make the breathless housewife churn;
And sometime make the drink to bear no barm;
Mislead night-wanderers, laughing at their harm?
Those that Hobgoblin call you and sweet Puck,
You do their work, and they shall have good luck:
Are not you he?

Puck

Thou speak'st aright;
I am that merry wanderer of the night.
I jest to Oberon and make him smile
When I a fat and bean-fed horse beguile,
Neighing in likeness of a filly foal:
And sometime lurk I in a gossip's bowl,
In very likeness of a roasted crab,
And when she drinks, against her lips I bob
And on her wither'd dewlap pour the ale.
The wisest aunt, telling the saddest tale,
Sometime for three-foot stool mistaketh me;
Then slip I from her bum, down topples she,
And 'tailor' cries, and falls into a cough;
And then the whole quire hold their hips and laugh,

And waxen in their mirth and neeze and swear
A merrier hour was never wasted there.
But, room, fairy! here comes Oberon.

~ William Shakespeare, A Midsummer Night's Dream

LUCAS MADE HIS WAY BACK TO THE VILLAGE. THE DISTANCE was not far, but it was steep. Lucas marched tiredly up and down the hills, the ungodly hour having finally caught up with him. He stopped to rest upon one high hilltop. There, he was able to see the lights of the Saint-Paul Asylum. They shone bright through the night, a beacon for the insane.

The asylum was something of a mystery to those in the village. Little was known of the staff, most of which lived on the grounds and kept to themselves. Less was known of the patients. Given how the night had so far gone, Lucas wondered if he might end up a patient himself come the break of day.

Lucas continued on his way, the countryside watchful with that secret commonwealth of elves, fauns, and fairies known to emerge on a midsummer's eve. Lucas couldn't see them. Few could. Such beings are not easily seen by those with the second sight, let alone a lamplighter. But Lucas was no ordinary lamplighter. He was the last lamplighter.

Lucas was making his way up a steadily sloping

hill near to the village when he came upon a fairy ring. A fairy ring is a place where mischievous spirits revel on moonlit nights. Fairy rings have been all but lost to memory in the modern age, but back then they were known by all to be wicked places that were best avoided. Old wives' tales told of hapless travelers entering fairy rings with dire consequences.

Lucas was well aware of fairy rings and their danger. He would have avoided the ritual if he could. Unfortunately, his duty would not allow it. He had no choice but to enter the ring, there being an unlit street lamp in the center. The spirits danced steadily around it as if in worship.

Lucas crept carefully up the hill for a closer look. A pale lord, perhaps the ghost of some long-dead Carolingian noble, paraded around the ring with a train of fairy subjects in tow. The faded apparition of a woman, perhaps a baroness from the same era, hummed a haunting melody, her voice rising and falling with the wind. The gathering was shrouded in a fog confined only to the ring. The moon shone upon them like a spotlight, as if it were all a scene from some dreamful play.

Lucas soon felt as though he were an unwilling participant in the dream. He lost all control of his body and found himself walking toward the fairy ring to join in the ritual. He came upon the circle without being noticed.

Lucas joined the band of fairies, dancing round and round in a heedless trance. He danced about as well as any lamplighter. That is to say, not well. He looked ridiculous. He looked and felt more marionette than man. He had little control of his movements. Who the puppeteer was, Lucas had no idea, but some sorcery had certainly possessed him.

He hadn't been dancing for long when the revelry came to an abrupt end. The singing stopped. The fairies disappeared. The mist blew away with the Mistral. All that remained was a nimbus of moonlight. It shone upon Lucas as he stood there dumbfounded.

Lucas felt as though he'd just woken from one of those elusive dreams, barely remembered. The enchanted ring was gone, as was the lamp within. A bare, decrepit tree stood where the street lamp had been, its bones creaking in the wind. Lucas felt a sense of relief at having survived the strange ordeal before continuing on his way. The village was then just a short walk away, over some small hills.

As Lucas ascended each hill he could see the village of Saint-Rémy, phosphorescent in the fading starlight. He could see the lights from some of the houses and smell the smoke from their chimneys. The night was no longer young. The lamplighter could tell its age from the sinking of the moon, soon to be swallowed by the hills.

LUCAS HAD NOT TRAVELED FAR FROM THE FAIRY RING WHEN he realized something was wrong. Although he walked toward the village, he came no nearer to it. The hills he climbed seemed to move backward as he moved forward. At each hilltop, the village remained the same distance away.

Lucas walked determinedly on, always following the moon. He trusted the moon more than his own senses. The moon was not deceitful. It played no tricks. It always hung lazily over the village late in the summer evenings. The moon had always been his midnight beacon.

He hummed that familiar nursery rhyme to himself as he walked:

The Man in the Moon looked out of the moon,
    Looked out of the moon and said,
    Tis time that, now I'm getting up,
    All children are in bed

"It is made of green cheese, you know," Lucas was startled by a voice from behind him.

He turned around, surprised to see before him a heavily bearded, elderly man with a bundle of sticks on his back. The old man carried a lantern in one hand and a cane in the other.

"The moon, I mean. It is made of green cheese," the old man repeated.

"I have heard such things," responded Lucas, not realizing the jest. For all he knew, the moon could have been made of Munster. He was just a lamplighter, after all.

"Who are you, grandfather, and why are you out and about at such an hour?"

"I am the Man in the Moon. As for my being out and about, I was just gathering firewood. It is cold as Christmas on the moon. It is also quite lonely. Tell me of yourself and why you wander these barren hills in the middle of the night."

"I am the lamplighter of the village," Lucas pointed toward the village. "The one your moon makes glow."

"What is a lamplighter doing still wandering about? Your lamps should have been lit long ago."

"I have gone and got myself lost. You see, I came upon a fairy ring not far back..."

"Ah," the old man interrupted, "and now you find yourself unable to leave the hills?"

"Well, yes. I walk the same way over and over again, getting no closer to the village."

"Consider yourself lucky. That clan of roguish imps have cast far worse spells on the unfortunate few who violate their marches. Freedom from such night magic requires help. Come, I will walk with you a while. We shall see if we can't find your way out of this curse."

Lucas continued slowly up and down the hills. The Man in the Moon followed close behind. He was in no rush, stopping now and then to pick up a twig for his lunar stove.

"I was not always so old, you know," the old man explained. "There was a time I looked much like you; young, strong, an endless life ahead of me. But now I am fading. I am fading with the rest of the night."

"Why is it that you fade?" asked Lucas.

"Day has broadened its reach. Civilization has seen to that with all these mechanized rays of light popping up out of nowhere. Soon, such lights will conquer the night altogether and with it the human imagination. What then?"

"I will certainly be out of business," said the lamplighter.

"As will I. There is no respect for a full moon with millions upon millions of imposter moons in existence. I think in a few short years I will be no more than a lonely, decorative orb."

"Not for me," consoled Lucas. "Not for the farmers, who harvest with your light late into the autumn evenings. Not for the hunters, whose prey you reveal in the fields. Not for the lovers, for whom you show the way."

"Thank you," smiled the old man. "Maybe I will survive a little while longer, if only in memory."

It wasn't long before the pair came upon the location of the fairy ring. The old man examined the stones, trees, and grasses as though it were a crime scene and he the detective.

"I know this place," explained the Man in the Moon. "I have shone upon spirits on this hill. Without the moonlight, their magic is ineffectual. I will return to the moon and draw a curtain for you. That will set you on your way. I should be returning home anyway. It is getting late."

"Thank you," said Lucas.

"Farewell, lamplighter. Do not wander this way again when the moon shines full upon a lingering summer's eve. There are strange sights to be had on such nights."

Strange sights indeed. The old man shuffled up and into the atmosphere on a staircase made of moonbeams. The wind waved his long, grey beard all about like the tail of a kite as he made his way higher and higher into the sky. It wasn't long before he disappeared entirely, just another dot among the stars.

Shortly after he disappeared, so did the moon. A band of thick clouds concealed it. As promised, the old man had drawn a curtain for the lamplighter. Lucas hurried on his way, hopeful the curtain would remain drawn and the fairy spell broken.

58

Lucas was relieved when he finally reached the main road leading into the village. The clouds then passed, the moon returning for a little while. It shone particularly bright upon an object off to the side of the road, as if to draw Lucas's attention to it.

It was a street lamp.

Lucas was pleasantly surprised to find his lamplighter's pole leaning on it. The tip of the pole was already lit as if it knew he was coming. Lucas grabbed hold of it and lit the lamp. For a moment, all seemed normal. Lucas had returned to the village, to his lamp-lighting ways.

"Surely, the strangest of this night is behind me," thought Lucas.

"Surely."

Have you ever heard the story of the old Street Lamp? It's really not very amusing, but you might listen to it for once.

It was such an honest lamp, which had done its duty for many, many years and which was now going to be discarded. It was the last evening it hung on its post and gave light to the street beneath it. The Lamp felt like an old ballet dancer who is performing for the last time and who knows that tomorrow she will be in a cold garret. The Lamp dreaded the morrow, for then it was to appear in the town hall and be inspected by the thirty-six council members, to see whether or not it was fit for further service.

It would be decided whether in the future the Lamp was to give light for the inhabitants of some suburb, or perhaps for some manufacturing plant in the country. But it might go at once to be melted down in an iron foundry! In that case it might become anything, but the Lamp was terribly troubled wondering whether, in some new state, it would remember it had once been a Street Lamp. In any case, the Lamp would be separated from the watchman and his wife, whom it had come to consider part of its family. It became a Lamp at the same time that he became a watchman.

*~ **The Old Street Lamp, Hans Christian Andersen, 1847***

Lucas walked into town, hopeful to find the rest of the lost lamps and finish his last night of work. By then, it was that ambiguous time of night which is considered either very late or very early. The evening would soon come to an end. Lucas must be getting home. He was tired. His daughter would soon awaken and expect him at her side.

Lucas walked the friendless streets, his only company the Mistral. She was more wind than woman, blowing hard as ever, sometimes quenching his lamplighter's pole. Lucas came upon a stray street lamp here or there, always in some unexpected corner or alleyway. He was encouraged with each new lamp he found, hopeful he might find more.

Lucas had not been at work in the village for long when he was surprised by the sight of what he first guessed to be a colossal man, at least ten-feet tall. The giant strolled casually down the middle of the street, taking impossibly long strides toward the center of town.

Lucas trailed the thing from a safe distance. At

first, it looked like the Ghost of Christmas Yet-to-Come. It was dark as the unlit streets. It was hunched over and skinny. Very skinny. Skinny as a lamp post. Lucas hadn't followed the figure for long before realizing it *was* a lamp post.

Lucas followed the living lamp until it reached the church at the center of town. The lamp ducked its monstrous glass head under the doors and walked inside. Lucas couldn't help but follow. He would like to meet a lamp and perhaps to light it. He was still a lamplighter, after all.

The church was one of those supremely strange and secret medieval cathedrals. It looked even stranger than usual that night. The stone edges were curved and, in some places, distorted. The color of the stone was swirled and smeared in certain spots, like a post-impressionist painting come to life. Two tall arched doors of gleaming wood with golden strap hinges made one think there must be something important inside, something unexpected. There was.

Lucas followed the lamp inside. He had expected the place to be empty at such a late (or early) hour, but it was not. It was filled, but not with people. A bespectacled gargoyle played "Moonlight Sonata" on the organ. Little angels fluttered around the sanctuary lamp like a swarm of holy honeybees. Moses sat in a pew, reading stories about himself from the Old Testament. Figures within the stained-glass windows came to life, reenacting whatever biblical scene they found themselves in.

The lamp strode to the front of the church. It knelt before a candlelit alter, bowing its immense head in prayer. Lucas made his way as inconspicuously as possible down the center aisle. He nodded to Moses, who paid him no mind. No one paid him any mind, with the exception of one of the stained glass depictions. It was the three wise men who noticed him. They lifted their crowned heads from baby Jesus in his manger, a look of wonder on their faces at the sight of the lamplighter. Lucas wondered why they were so surprised. Surely there was at least one lamplighter in Bethlehem.

Lucas knelt next to the lamp, who was in deep prayer. Lucas pretended to pray himself, always keeping a side eye on the lamp. He waited impatiently for the lamp to finish so that he might introduce himself. But the minutes passed, with the lamp showing no signs of stopping.

"Ahem, excuse me, sir," Lucas interrupted the lamp. "Would you happen to have a light? I should like to light a votive candle."

The lamp looked down on the lamplighter with eyes wide in recognition.

"I should think a lamplighter would have himself a match at all times," spoke the lamp with a voice so deep it seemed to come from the crypt. "It is your duty to light fires, is it not?"

"Ah, then we've met," smiled Lucas. "I thought I recognized you. Are you the lamp from Lafayette Street?"

"Certainly not! I stand at the corner of Saint Joseph Street and Andre Avenue." The lamp was clearly offended at being mistaken for another lamp from another street.

"Who are you lighting a candle for?" the lamp asked.

"For the soul of my wife," answered Lucas. He often lit prayer candles for his wife.

"In that case, here you are," the lamp handed Lucas a book of matches. "You are rather young for a widower."

"The youngest in the village, but this is a small village. Tell me, what brings a street lamp to church so late at night?" Lucas asked as he lit his candle. "Shouldn't you be out, shining?"

"What brings anyone to church?" responded the lamp. "I am praying."

"As am I," lied Lucas. "Might I ask what it is a lamp prays for?"

"I am praying for my own soul and those of my brethren. You of all people must know the fires of all the street lamps in the village will be forever quenched tomorrow. Technology, electricity, machinery... These things are the way of the future. Tonight is the last night of my life. I am afraid."

"What are you afraid of? Dying?" Lucas asked. Recently widowed, the lamplighter considered himself an expert on the subject.

"Well, yes. I am afraid of the oblivion, the nothingness, the permanent extinguishment of my own flame."

"Oblivion is nothing to fear because it is nothing whatsoever," explained Lucas. "One can have no experience, but experience. And who is to say you will not have another experience? Perhaps you will wake up one day a giant-sized, fancily shaped lamp in downtown London, with no remembrance of your life as a little flame on Saint Joseph Street in the south of France."

The lamp was keenly interested in the lamplighter's perspective.

"You presume the nothingness I fear is a deception?" asked the lamp.

"I do. Nothingness is a hoax, and an absurd one at that. There is no absence of being, at least no experience of it."

"What of my flame?" the lamp countered. "Certainly, that will be gone. What do you say to that?"

"You will still spread light, just from a different source. You will be electronic. I have heard mechanized lights are in some cases brighter than whole bonfires."

"The mechanization of fire is a curse upon the night," declared the lamp. "It is unnatural."

"You may be right," acknowledged Lucas.

The two sat in silence a while, before Lucas worked up the courage to ask one final question.

"There is precious little darkness left in this night. May I light your fire, one last time?"

"Yes, of course," agreed the lamp. "Walk with me to my corner of Saint Joseph Street. I would like to end this last night where I began my first one when this village was little more than a crossroads."

The two rose from the alter. Lucas followed the lamp as he proceeded down the center aisle. The three wise men once again stopped their praying to observe the lamplighter. A statue of Saint Christopher wished them safe travels as they passed through the narthex and into the night.

Lucas and the lamp proceeded down the dark, desolate streets. The peculiar pair would have been quite the sight to behold were there anyone to see them. The village was not yet awake.

That time when the earliest of risers stirred was Lucas's favorite time of night (or morning). At that hour, the lamplighter was normally at work extinguishing all the street lamps for the coming day[1]. He roamed the town, captivated with all the nothingness. At times, he felt as though he was the only man on earth. That sense of being alone did not make him feel lonely. It made him feel free. He smiled as he worked. Sometimes he sang a tune all alone in the middle of some empty street, as though no one were watching. But the lamps had seen it all.

The two soon reached that corner where the lamp had stood all his life.

"I shone for many a midnight wanderer, didn't I?" asked the lamp.

"Truly, you shone like none other," consoled Lucas. "You shone for me."

The lamp stood in quiet contemplation a few seconds. He would go to sleep as he always had, hopeful to wake again. After all, waking was the only possibility according to the lamplighter.

"Do your duty lamplighter. I am cold. The wind whirls and twirls like a music-box ballerina on this night. A fire would be helpful."

The lamp stood straight and still. He closed his eyes one last time, unafraid. Shortly after he closed his eyes, they vanished altogether. The lamp's arms and legs stiffened until they once again became the cold, curved steel Lucas was used to.

Lucas snapped a match to life and lit his pole. He reached up and carefully ignited the lamp.

That was a solemn, farewell fire. Lucas felt as

though he hadn't lit an ordinary street lamp but a sacred candle. He was right. It was no simple street lamp. It was a street lamp he had known his whole life, one that had burned since time immemorial. His father had once lit it, as had his father before him. It was the street lamp at the corner of Saint Joseph Street and Andre Avenue.

"Electricity again!" he exclaimed, and fled.

Notre-Dame was ahead of him, its windows streaming with light; solemn chanting was audible as Michel entered the old cathedral. Mass was just ending. Leaving the darkness of the streets, Michel was dazzled: the altar shone with electric light, and beams from the same source escaped from the monstrance raised in the priest's hand. "More electricity," the miserable boy exclaimed, "even here!" And once more he fled, but not so quickly that he failed to hear the organ roaring with compressed air furnished by the Catacomb Company! Michel was going mad; he believed the demon of electricity was pursuing him, and he returned to the Quai de Gréves, entering a labyrinth of empty streets until he came out into the Place des Vosges, where a statue of Victor Hugo had replaced that of Louis XV, and found himself facing the new Boulevard Napoleon IV, which extended to the square where Louis XIV perpetually gallops toward the Banque de France; making a hairpin turn, he came back along the Rue Notre-Dame des Victoires.

~ Jules Verne, Paris in the Twentieth Century, 1860

LUCAS LEFT THE LAMP, CONTINUING HIS SEARCH OF THE village for those remaining ones in need of lighting. He would find more, hidden here and there in the most unexpected of places. One stood watchfully on the roof of the blacksmith shop. Another lay lost in a ditch on the side of the road. He found several standing in a circle near to the graveyard, as if in mourning.

Lucas continued until he had lit nearly all of the village lamps. Had he been an amateur lamplighter he may have returned home then, without having lit all the lamps in the village. But Lucas was no amateur. He was the consummate professional, and having lit the lamps for so long, he knew when the job was finished. There was one last lamp to be lit.

Lucas searched the village high and low for that last elusive lamp. He walked the same silent streets, again and again. He checked and double-checked the barren back alleys. He tramped through quiet gardens. He crept up to cottages, peeking through their dark windows like a thief in the night. The lamp was nowhere to be found.

Lucas was left no choice but to leave the village, searching once again through the farms and fields on its outskirts. He hurried along, knowing the earliest of risers would soon be awake. Dawn was not far off. Lucas could see it in the dew on the grass. He could hear it in the birdsong. He could smell it in the earth returning to life. More than anything, he could feel it in his weary bones. Never had he spent the whole night at work.

Just when Lucas was about to give up on the last lamp, he was stopped by a voice. The voice was unexpected, not only because of the hour, but because of its sound and source. It was a low voice, but it came from on high – very high. It was the voice of that renowned cypress tree, front and center in *The Starry Night*.

"You look lost," observed the tree.

Lucas faced the tree. Ghostly green eyes shone from within the topmost branches where the shape of a head formed. Its face was tree-lichen covered beneath a thick, red beard. Long hair made of leaves dangled in the wind. Out of its head sprouted two horn-like branches.

"I am not lost," Lucas looked up. "I am looking for something lost."

"What have you lost?"

"I am the lamplighter. There is one last lamp I cannot seem to find. Have you seen a stray lamp in these parts?"

"Here? No. A lamp has not stood here since the monks made the monastery."

"The monastery was built hundreds of years ago. Are you so old?" Lucas asked. "I didn't know trees lived so long."

"I am older than most, but not all," the cypress explained. "There is a cedar grove up in the mountains, which may be older than the mountains themselves. Some trees live many hundreds of years. Others no more than a few."

Lucas and the tree stared at one another in curious silence.

"I remember you," said the tree. "When you were a boy, you climbed on my back and played among my branches, as did your father, and his father before him."

The tree was right. Lucas looked at it more closely and recognized it, a long-lost childhood friend.

"I remember you," said Lucas. "It has been awhile. I am glad to see you once more, as I did when I was young."

"Where is the girl you played with?" asked the tree. "The one who danced in my branches."

"Chloe? She is asleep," lied Lucas, not knowing exactly why he was lying.

Perhaps he was lying not to upset the tree. Lucas and Chloe had done more than play in the branches of the tree. They had passed countless summer afternoons there, laughing, playing, talking over those fantasies of childhood. The place itself was a kind of fantasy. That is what trees are for children. They are pillars of make-believe, meant for the exchange of secret dreams, among other things. That tree was no different.

"I see," the tree squinted with doubt. "You may not have seen me all this time, but I have seen you.

You pass this way every night on your way to light those lamps nearest the canal. I see you marching through the twilight fields, torch in hand, the cockcrow schoolboy turned man of midnight."

"You will see me no more. After tonight, there will be no lamplighter. The village is being wired for electricity."

"Electrici-what? I have heard whispers in the wind of such black magic. The lighting of lamps without fire, paddling of boats without paddles, horse-drawn carriages without horses... Such news does not bode well for the village."

"It does not bode well for me," added Lucas. "What purpose will I have in the world?"

"What is the purpose of anything?" asked the cypress back.

Lucas had no answer. He was just a lamplighter, after all.

"This road you walk is older than even me," the tree explained. "I have spoken with its many travelers, each with their own purpose. I have met priests of many faiths, who all claimed the same purpose: to love and serve whatever god they worship. I once met a sage from the orient, who explained there was no god, and that life has no purpose, reason, or choice. The first of the Frankish kings camped under my eaves. His purpose was power. Not so his queen. She was a mother. A mother's meaning, whether sovereign or slave, is always the same — to protect her children."

"Was there some all-knowing traveler who knew our truest purpose?" asked Lucas.

"The wisest man I ever met was a fig farmer. I asked him the meaning of life, naturally expecting him to claim it was farming figs. He asked me why I, or anyone else for that matter, would care at all what his answer was. He said the question itself was no different than asking what his favorite color was. The absolute truth of the answer was his alone. I believe the fig farmer was right. Each of us has our own meaning."

"What is meaning for you, a tree?" asked Lucas.

"Meaning for me is dancing with the wind," answered the tree without hesitation.

The Mistral blew hard as ever as if in answer to the cypress. The old tree swayed and bent crazily, its branches flailing all about. It was dancing.

The wind settled as suddenly as it had started and the unusual conversation continued.

"What is meaning for you, a lamplighter?"

"I am no philosopher, but I think meaning changes over time. Meaning as a boy was climbing your limbs, pretending to fly from them. Meaning as a man is a home, with children, and a fire on a night as windy as this one. Meaning for me on this night is work and finding the last lamp."

"Perhaps I can help you find your meaning on this night," offered the cypress. "You say the last lamp is nowhere to be found. Where is it normally found?"

"What does it matter where the lamp is normally found?" countered Lucas. "All the lamps have gone astray. Some I have found as far afield as the river valley. The last lamp could be anywhere."

"I should think there is one lamp," the tree explained, "a lamp so important that it could never be moved, not by the hand of god. It is a lamp which fate meant for you to discover last of all — the last lamp of the last lamplighter. Why should it not be where you might easily find it?"

The last lamp was normally found in an unusual spot. It sat at the end of a narrow, seldom used alley on the edge of town. The lamp had once lit the entrance to a tannery, long since closed. The forsaken lamp served no real purpose to the townsfolk, but it did serve a purpose to Lucas. Being the last lamp, it was where he often met his wife after his shift ended.

"I will see about that lamp," said Lucas to the cypress. "I am happy to have rediscovered you, old friend. Perhaps I will return on some quiet, starry night to philosophize, or climb."

"I think there will never be another night so quiet and starry as this one. I fear the haze of cold electric lights will consume the burgundy and blue of eventide, eventually drowning out the stars themselves."

"I hope you are wrong. Without the stars, what will stir our spirits? What will become of us all, without the stargazers?"

"We will become worse, but that is not your concern tonight. Go now. Light your last lamp. There may be someone needing it to find their way home. It is still dark for a little while."

"Farewell, cypress."

"Farewell, lamplighter."

Lucas made his way back to the village. It was not far.

Before he entered the confines of the town, he turned back around to the countryside. He hoped for one more look at the thoughtful cypress. The hillsides were barren. The farmers slept a while longer, but the morning Mistral had awoken. She blew hard and heavy over the fields.

Lucas saw the cypress in the distance, a wiry silhouette against the predawn sky. The old tree opened its branches wide, welcoming the wind. The cypress swayed here and there and all around, dancing with the wind as if it were his purpose in life. And it was.

It certainly is a strange phenomenon that all the artists, poets, musicians, painters, are unfortunate in material things — the happy ones as well — what you said lately about Guy de Maupassant is a fresh proof of it. That brings up again the eternal question: is life completely visible to us, or isn't it rather that this side of death we see one hemisphere only?

Painters — to take them only — being dead and buried, speak to the next generation or to several succeeding generations through their work.

Is that all, or is there more besides? In a painter's life death is not perhaps the hardest thing there is.

For my own part, I declare I know nothing whatever about it. But to look at the stars always makes me dream, as simply as I dream over the black dots of a map representing towns and villages. Why, I ask myself, should the shining dots of the sky not be as accessible as the black dots on the map of France? If we take the train to get to Tarascon or Rouen, we take death to reach a star. One thing undoubtedly true in this reasoning is this: that while we are alive we cannot get to a star, any more than when we are dead we can take the train.

So it doesn't seem impossible to me that cholera, gravel, pleurisy & cancer are the means of celestial locomotion, just as steam-boats, omnibuses and railways are the terrestrial means. To die quietly of old age would be to go there on foot.

Now I am going to bed, because it is late, and I wish you good night and good luck.

A handshake, Yours
    Vincent

~ **Vincent Van Gogh Letter to brother Theo, July 1888**

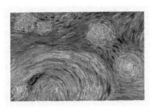

LUCAS HURRIED THROUGH THE VILLAGE STREETS. HE HAD precious little time. Signs of the coming morning were all around. Dogs barked at the remnants of raccoons. Barn owls hooted at the last of the moon. Cottages breathed smoke from chimneys. Candlelight flickered to life in some of the windows. Church bells would soon clang in the belfry, announcing the start of a new day.

Lucas reached the all-too-familiar alleyway, relieved to see the last lamp at its end. The alley was still quite dark. Lucas lit his pole to light the way.

Strangely, the torch did not help to light the way. The alley actually became darker as Lucas walked down it toward the lamp. The stone wall to his left was consumed by night. The house to his right faded to black. Even the street under him would soon disappear.

By the time Lucas reached the end of the alley, there was nothing left but the lamp. And there was nothing left for Lucas to do but light the lamp. The moment he did, colors began to emerge from the darkness all around. Straw yellow stars blinked to life like holes poked in a black lamp shade. The moon took shape, as did the rest of that luminous night.

Lucas found himself standing on a span of stardust, somewhere between the Big and Little Dipper with the rest of the galaxy all around. The

Mistral welcomed him, running her cold fingers through his hair one last time before blowing out to sea. Lucas saw the old fisherman, still sailing through the Milky Way after his long-lost mermaid. They were far away by then, somewhere near Mars maybe. Lucas saw the Man in the Moon, waving from a window with his night cap on, preparing himself for bed.

Far below Lucas was the village of Saint-Rémy. He looked down and saw the streets and canals crisscrossing the town, dotted with all the lamps he had lit that night and so many other nights before. There was the spire of the old church, its stained-glass windows alive with color. Lucas saw the rows of ancient cypresses whirling back and forth in the wind. Beyond the village, the hills of the countryside rose and fell like immense waves in an unfathomable sea.

Lucas's attention was soon drawn back to the sky, to a woman. She was dancing all alone, not far from where he stood. She wore a faded summer dress. Lucas knew that dress. The woman who wore it had only a handful of dresses to her name. It hung long and loose on her, all the way down to her slippers. On her head was the crown of poppies she often wore in the summertime.

It was his wife, Chloe. Lucas shouted for her.

She smiled at him as though she were still alive, as though it were just another night. She signaled for him to come closer, to ignite the stars all around her as if they were street lamps in need of lighting. Dawn was fading them.

Lucas walked weightlessly through what was left of the night. He reached up with his lamplighters pole as if it were a magic wand, setting fire to the stars.

The stars came to life after they were lit. Some sang. Others smiled. Most danced with Chloe, who encouraged Lucas to keep kindling, to keep the night alive. He did, and there was never a lamplighter who performed his duties with such fervor.

Lucas lit stars near and far, of all shapes and sizes and eons. He lit red and brown dwarfs, blue giants and bright giants. He lit stars from the dawn of the universe. He lit newborn stars no older than him. He even lit Mercury on fire, mistaking it for star.

Lucas carried on with his star-lighting until it seemed there were whole constellations whirling about his wife. There were serpents, scorpions, jinns, jackalopes, and hippocamps. The pale gleam of a hero hunted them all. A jeweled giant skipped asteroids through the milk of the Milky Way. A winged unicorn soared through the night, its tail that of a comet.

Chloe laughed and danced in the midst of it all. Her white dress blew so wildly in the wind Lucas thought she might blow away altogether. She didn't. She hiked up her dress, tapping those spectral slippers on the night. The strange thing about that tap was *how* it tapped. It struck the sky like not-so-faraway thunder every time she tapped it. The thunder rumbled on even after she was done tapping, as she do-si-doed around the stars. The stars were aware of her, growing fuller and larger, moving toward her and with her, twirling in and around her as if the whole scene was choreographed.

Chloe danced her way to Lucas, smiling an invitation to join her. He knew she was only teasing him, as she used to. Lucas was no dancer. He was a lamplighter. She spun slowly away from him, sashaying with the pajama-wearing Man in the Moon instead.

When the lightning began, Chloe started moving faster and more frantically. She was twisting and turning, hooting and hollering all throughout the stratosphere like some mad, ghostly contortionist. She stopped when the rain started. It came down slowly at first. Chloe held her palms out and up, catching the first drops like a surprised child.

Soon it was pouring, and there was something strange about that rain. It was gradually blurring everything around Lucas and not because it was coming down so hard and heavy. That rain came down like the silver strokes of some cosmological paintbrush, painting over the whole world. The village below had already disappeared, as had the countryside.

Lucas watched Chloe. She stood all alone in the rain, fading with the stars. Morning was finally at-hand. Lucas realized then that the night was over and that something must be done.

The rain fell harder and faster as Lucas rushed toward Chloe. By the time he reached her most everything around them was gone. Despite the rain, Chloe was dry as ever. She smiled at Lucas and said something, but the words fell away with the rain. Everything was becoming dim and distorted. Chloe looked imaginary. Lucas reached out to touch her, wiping the freckles from her face like specks of clay. Her eyes gleamed, but he couldn't decide on their color. They changed with the brightening sky. Black. Brown. Blue. Her hair curled and uncurled before his eyes, falling straight down to her shoulders, before bouncing back up again. The crown of poppies shone from her head like a halo, like an angel from a nursery rhyme.

Then Lucas kissed her. It wasn't a lusty, enchanted kiss of the sort that cures cancer or raises the dead. Lucas was no prince. He was a lamplighter. As for Chloe, she may have been a princess, but only in absinthe-induced fantasies. Only in dreams.

No, that kiss was not of the fairy-tale sort. It was a good-bye kiss, granted by those secret divinities of the stars. The kiss may have come from the great beyond, but it tasted like the real thing. It tasted like the break of day.

THE GARDENER

THE SUN PEEKED OVER THE EASTERN HORIZON, SPILLING summer over the farms and fields. The starry night retreated west and into the annals of art history. Morning shone upon the village of Saint-Rémy all at once as though a switch had been flicked. The age of flicking switches had arrived. An engineer would soon arrive from Paris to wire switches for flicking — cold, electric lights to forever dim the stars.

The sunrise would not wake Lucas. Nor would the church bells, nor the sound of his daughter preparing for school. The former lamplighter slept one of those deep, dreamless sleeps. He need not rise to put out the lamps. The rain and wind had done that for him. His job was forever done.

Down the old road from the village, past the rows of older cypresses, the Saint Paul Asylum was waking. A doctor recorded his appointments for the day. The sisters watered plants in the garden. A chef cooked breakfast. Orderlies wandered the halls, checking on patients.

Patient Vincent Van Gogh had been awake before all the rest. He was not awake to paint. He had tried to paint the night before. He could not paint in the dark. He was awake to watch, so that he might paint the predawn sky from memory and imagination, during the day.

Vincent looked out his east-facing window at the fading night, more richly colored than the day. He memorized the positions of the stars, moon, and the rolling hills of the countryside. They would all make for important elements in his painting. But there was more to the night. What about the luminosity of it all? Or the wind? What about that sleepy village near to the asylum?

He could not see the village, but he could imagine it. There was the church, its spire a lance through the heavens. There were the cottages, their windows glowing gold from oil lamps to balance that shimmer within the stars above. The oil lamps would also suggest a human presence. Vincent wondered who the townsfolk were and how they lived.

Vincent would finish his legendary landscape in just a few days. He was dismissive of the painting, referring to it as a 'study.' He would later send it to his brother Theo in Paris, who was also critical of the painting, notably its exaggerated portrayal of the night sky.

For the next fifty years *The Starry Night* would remain largely hidden from the public eye as it passed between private owners and collections. It was eventually brought to New York by Paul Rosenberg, a Jewish art dealer fleeing Nazi occupied France. Rosenberg traded the painting to the Museum of Modern Art where it quickly gained renown. It still hangs there today.

LATER THAT SAME SUMMER AT THE ASYLUM VINCENT FLED down the hallway. He was fleeing not only from the voice in his head but those of his neighbors. The mentally ill residents were often unruly. They were especially so on that day.

Vincent arrived at the garden, his place of refuge and inspiration. Being late summer, it was still blooming with every color imaginable. Vincent walked the familiar path to his favorite stone bench. The bench sat below a row of pine trees. The trees bent back and forth, wailing a welcome in the wind.

Vincent removed the clay pipe from his pocket to smoke and settle his mind. He needed a light. Patients were not allowed matches, for obvious reasons. He looked around the garden for someone who might help. The carriage driver who normally assisted him was nowhere to be found.

Vincent was surprised to see a new face wandering the garden. It was that of a young man. The man was tall and skinny, standing straight and rigid as a pole. His dark hair and lampshade mustache were a coal black. His eyes were a smoldering shade of grey. He wore a raggedy straw hat like a rain shield. He had a friendly face, and disposition.

Vincent waved to the man, signaling for him to come closer. The man put down his gardening tools and reluctantly made his way to the one-eared patient.

"Pardon me sir, but we have not met," said Vincent. "Are you new here?"

"I am," the man responded. "I have only just started today. I am the new gardener."

"Welcome to you, gardener. I come here often and will be glad to have you. The garden is beautiful, but it has become quite overgrown. Look at the ivy covering the grass, creeping up the pines."

"I know it," agreed the gardener. "If something is not done, the weeds will soon suffocate the lilacs."

"That would be a tragedy! I painted the lilacs when I first arrived."

"You are an artist then?" asked the man. "What do you paint?"

"I am indeed an artist. I paint most anything. I have very much liked to paint this garden. I paint the pines and poppies. I paint the almond trees. I paint the wind waving the branches."

"I should like to see your work," said the gardener. "If I were an artist I would paint the night, but only for myself. Working all day in the garden, I expect to see very little of the evening."

"I have painted the night from my window there on the second floor," Van Gogh pointed up to his room. "It is a majestic view."

"It looks to be," agreed the gardener.

They were interrupted by a howl of utmost lunacy from within the asylum. The howl reminded Vincent why he had come to the garden. He had come to relax, to smoke. But he still needed a light.

"Would you happen to have a light, kind sir?" Vincent asked, holding up his pipe. "Patients are not permitted fire."

"Of course," said the gardener, removing a book of matches from his breast pocket. He ignited one with a simple snap of his fingers and handed it to Vincent with a smile.

"Thank you," said Vincent. "You certainly know how to light a fire. Is that a parlor trick?"

The gardener nodded before turning back to his work in the weeds.

"What did you say your name was?" Vincent asked.

"Lucas. And yours?"

"Vincent."

"Pleasure to make your acquaintance, Vincent. If you'll excuse me, I must get back to work."

<hr />

LUCAS TENDED HIS GARDEN. VINCENT PAINTED IT. Daylight faded swift as a dull memory. The madness of the asylum was soon quieted by sleep, as was the nearby village of Saint-Rémy. Watchful stars blinked to life without a lamplighter to watch them back.

Someone watched them back. Someone still watches them.

Who? Perhaps the last lighthouse keeper, peering over the expanse of invisible sea, a perfect mirror for the stars. Maybe a lonely soldier, longing for home. Maybe a writer, face creased with sleep, staring from some bedroom window. Maybe you, whoever, wherever you are.

The Gardener, Vincent Van Gogh 1889, painted two months after The Starry Night, from within the Saint Remy Asylum

AUTHOR'S NOTE

Thank you for reading. I hope you liked it. I hope Van Gogh would have liked it. I think he would have. He was a strange bird. This is a story for strange birds.

If you enjoyed the book, please leave a review online. I'm an independent author, with no marketing or public relations support from a traditional publisher. Online reviews are important in helping to connect me with readers like you.

If you'd like to receive future notifications of upcoming titles, subscribe to my mailing list at https://www.absurdistfiction.com/. I often send out advanced reader copies of new books to that mailing list.

I wish you good night and good luck...

ABOUT THE AUTHOR

Steve is a purveyor of the finest in speculative literature from Chicago. He has authored five novels, and his short fiction has been published everywhere from *Crannóg* magazine in Galway, Ireland, to *Papercuts* magazine in Pakistan. Steve once passionately kissed a bronze seahorse in the middle of Buckingham Fountain. Seriously, he did.

For new title release and other information, visit Steve's author website at https://www.absurdistfiction.com/.

You can email Steve at lavenderlinepress@gmail.com.

WORK CITED

- Andersen, H. C. (Hans Christian) and Charles Boner. *Fairy Tales.* New York: Allen, 1869, https://catalog.hathitrust.org/Record/011556332/Home. Accessed 22 June 2023.
- Buck, Stephanie. "During a 1994 Blackout, L.A. Residents Called 911 When They Saw the Milky Way for the First Time." *Medium*, 16 Feb. 2017, https://timeline.com/los-angeles-light-pollution-ebd60d5acd43.
- Carroll, Lewis, et al. *Alice's Adventures in Wonderland.* Rand, McNally & Company, 1902. *HathiTrust*, https://catalog.hathitrust.org/Record/100543748. Accessed 22 June 2023.
- Hodara, Susan. "The City of Lights, When It Was First Lighted: [Metropolitan Desk]." *New York Times, Late Edition (East Coast)*, 5 June 2016, p. CT.8.Kipling, Rudyard. *Rewards and Fairies*. Doubleday, Page & Company, 1914. *HathiTrust*, https://catalog.hathitrust.org/Record/102752530. Accessed 22 June 2023.
- MacDonald, George. *At the Back of the North Wind*. A.L. Burt, Publisher, 189?. *HathiTrust*, https://catalog.hathitrust.org/Record/008666765. Accessed 22 June 2023.
- "Mermaid Rule Britannia." *Lyrics On Demand,* https://www.lyricsondemand.com/u/unknown-lyrics/mermaidrulebritannialyrics.html. Accessed 16 June 2023.

- PICRYL - Public Domain Media Search Engine. "Vincent Willem van Gogh 054 - Picryl - Public Domain Media Search Engine Public Domain Search." *PICRYL*, 1 Jan. 1600, picryl.com/media/vincent-willem-van-gogh-054-e4c690.

- Shakespeare, William. *A Midsummer-Night's Dream,* edited by A.W. Verity. 1905. *HathiTrust*, https://catalog.hathitrust.org/Record/100549460. Accessed 22 June 2023.

- Stevenson, Robert Louis. "The Lamplighter." *Robert Louis Stevenson Reader*, edited by Catherine T. Bryce, C. Scribner's Sons, 1906, p. 39. *HathiTrust*, https://catalog.hathitrust.org/Record/005959944. Accessed 22 June 2023.

- "To John Adams from Benjamin Rush, 17 October 1809," *Founders Online,* National Archives, https://founders.archives.gov/documents/Adams/99-02-02-5450. Accessed 22 June 2023.

- "To Theo van Gogh. Arles, Monday, 9 or Tuesday, 10 July 1888." *Vincent van Gogh Letters,* Van Gogh Museum, https://www.vangoghletters.org/vg/letters/let638/letter.html#translation. Accessed 16 June 2023.

- *Van Gogh the Starry Night - Public Domain Pictures*, www.publicdomainpictures.net/en/view-image.php?image=448920&picture=van-gogh-the-starry-night. Accessed 6 July 2023.

- Verne, Jules, and Richard Howard. *Paris in the Twentieth Century*. 1st U.S. ed., Random House, 1996.

- Wilde, Oscar. *The Writings of Oscar Wilde.* Gabriel Wells, 1925. *HathiTrust*, https://catalog.hathitrust.org/Record/009904727.

NOTES

CHAPTER 2

1. At the request of his brother Theo, Vincent was allowed a generous half-liter of wine with meals.

CHAPTER 5

1. Paris was first wired with electric street lights in 1878. Electricity astounded visitors at the Exposition Universelle of 1889 (world's fair) in the city where electric lights shone from the top of the newly constructed Eiffel Tower.
2. Scottish term for lamplighter

CHAPTER 15

1. Lamplighters were also lamp-extinguishers, having the responsibility of smothering fires in the mornings.